Robert Herrick

The Man Who Wins

Robert Herrick

The Man Who Wins

1st Edition | ISBN: 978-3-75237-614-2

Place of Publication: Frankfurt am Main, Germany

Year of Publication: 2020

Outlook Verlag GmbH, Germany.

THE MAN WHO WINS

BY

ROBERT HERRICK

I

The Four Corners in Middleton made a pleasant drive from the university town of Camberton. Many a time in the history of the house a party of young fellows had driven over the old turnpike that started where the arsenal used to stand in the sacred quarter of Camberton, and as the evening sun gilded the low, fresh-water marshes beyond Spring Pond, would trot on toward the rolling hills of Middleton. After dinner, or a dance, or, perhaps, mere chat over a late supper, they rode away at midnight singing as they whipped up their sleepy nags and otherwise disturbing the decorum of night in Middleton. Or, maybe, routed out early on a frosty October morning, after lighting pipes and a word with the stable-boy, they would snuggle into overcoats and spin away over the hard roads where the night frost still lay on the caked dust in the hollows like a crust of milk. In crossing the meadows the autumn sun swung into their faces, a comfortable solace on a morning drive, exciting them forward toward Camberton that they might report in the little stucco chapel while the tinny college bell was still harshly calling to prayer.

The Ellwells had kept the old Four Corners in Middleton long after the family had moved out into the wider world of Boston, and from farming and the ministry had entered the spheres of commerce and money-owning. In the time of old Roper Ellwell the Four Corners had been the parsonage for Middleton, and there first the Rev. Roper Ellwell had stirred the placid waters of meeting-house faith until something like a primitive revival had spread into neighboring parishes. His wife, a learned woman, had managed half a dozen young men who were preparing their Greek and Latin for Camberton. Those were the homely and kindly days of the Four Corners.

Then Roper Ellwell was called by the Second Church, in Boston, to be their pastor. This was the beginning of the Ellwell family in the good society of New England. The pastor's eloquence waxed into books that are found to-day on the shelves of the Harvard Library, with the University book-plate recording their gift by the author; also in black-cloth bindings, admirably printed, going to auction from some private library formed by a parishioner of the noted divine. When he became old in service, the congregation, now rich and fashionable, added to his ministrations the vigor of a younger man. Yet Roper Ellwell, on fine Sundays, still fired one of his former discourses from the lofty pulpit of his church. As these days grew rarer, the old pastor divided his time between his son's house on Beacon Street and the Four Corners.

Mark Ellwell was, as he should be, his father's son with the leaven of a newer world which led him into business instead of the ministry. But a fair product of Camberton, and a man well known and liked in Boston, where he was a merchant, when that term did not cover shop-keeping or gambling. He made a solid fortune in wool; built a house just beyond Charles Street on Beacon Street; was a member of two good clubs, and a deacon in his father's church.

In these days the Four Corners was used chiefly in the autumn months, and as a playhouse for the feeble pastor. Mark Ellwell built a summer home in Nahant.

There was one son who grew up—John. This Ellwell was sent to Camberton in due time, where he broke the family tradition by living a licentious life. He was kept in the university for two years, from respect to his family, in spite of his drunkenness and idleness. When the war broke out—John was then in his third year at Camberton—the wilder blood at the university found its field. Young Ellwell shirked his chance; while his mates were enlisting and leaving college, he slunk away in little sprees, pleading weak health. Mark Ellwell, shamed and mortified, would have horsewhipped his son into the ranks, but the mother defended the weakling.

One day young Ellwell announced his marriage to a Salem girl whom he had met the week before. His father gave him a house; as he chose to be a broker, his father started him with his own credit. A few years later, when the war was over and John Ellwell was succeeding in the general tide of success, established with a family and three young children, all seemed well. Now the Four Corners was rarely visited. The verandas broke down; grass and hardy roses grew into the cracks where the clap-boards had started. The Ellwells, father and son, were fashionable people; the family had developed.

Early in the seventies there came rumors of young Ellwell's disgrace in the Tremont Club. He was detected cheating at play, and left the club, of which Mark Ellwell was vice-president. John Ellwell was a large, florid man, with the fine features of the good New England pastor, a slightly Roman nose, and a gouty tendency in his walk. He was the flourishing broker, of the kind who worked on nerve, who was never sober after three in the afternoon, and having begun to drink at ten was uncertain after twelve. He knew a side of business life that his father had never seen; he associated with men whom the stiff Mark would have disdained to recognize. But his reputation for cleverness carried him on in spite of the club affair until....

One day, after a spree, he went on the Board wild and flurried. What he did he could never remember, but when the settlement for that day's transactions was made he was ruined. The Board gave him a week to find the necessary funds and pay his debts. His father settled the affair, opened the Four Corners for his family, sold his own house on Beacon Street, and taking his two daughters, who had never married, sailed for Europe. That was the end of the Ellwells in

3

old Boston. Mark Ellwell never came back.

"The old man is done with me." That had been John's comment to his wife. And well might Mark Ellwell be done with him; there was not much left for another clearing up. There were the Four Corners, and his seat in the Board, and then—beggary. So in the third generation the Ellwells established themselves once more in Middleton at the Four Corners.

II

Good people, people of fortunes nicely won and carefully transmitted, well-known people, in short the members of society who make life an important affair to be honorably transacted in due reverence for their own reputation and the opinion of their neighbors, had nothing more to do with the family. They were blotted out of the blue book of Boston and never ventured beyond the shady walks of the Common on the Beacon Street side. In the other world, about the exchange, in the bar-rooms and restaurants of the downtown hotels, John Ellwell still led a comfortable life. The Board liked him. His transactions never again assumed large proportions, but in the way of little things he did a brisk business and went his old, corrupt, uncertain path.

The old house at Middleton was pulled to pieces and made fit for a gentleman's family, with a comfortable dining-room and broad-bayed windows, fine mahogany from the Beacon Street house, and an opulent cellar. Wide verandas were run about the house again, giving delightful vine-covered nooks for talk and sewing in the hazy, heated summer days. The lawn was nicely shaved and watered; the drive that led through the orchard to the cross-roads which gave the name to the place was weeded and gravelled. A new stable was put up behind, and furnished with three horses, some smart little carts, besides a close carriage for rainy days. The exile was made tolerable— for the sake of the children.

Mrs. John Ellwell counted for little. She had married in romance the handsome, swell young man; reality had blasted her. She had sunk into a will-less invalid, and made admiration of her husband into pride and a religion. She had accepted; she never protested. The eldest son by the dint of much pushing had been put into Camberton just before the final smash and the exile. In the hall of the college there hung a portrait of his great grandfather in his black preacher's robes; of this, Roper Ellwell, second, was a weak travesty. The thin features had been blurred in the process of transmitting; an inclination to flabby stoutness of person made the young man portly, where the old minister had been nervously fragile. But Roper Ellwell, second, rarely compared notes, for he dined, not in hall under this picture, but at a private club with his own set.

These young fellows drove over now and then to the Four Corners, a pleasant place for a man to spend an evening or a Sunday when the weather was fair and the fields green. The dinners were long and rich; the wines good; and if old Ellwell was a somewhat scandalous host, pleasing only to the coarser lads, there were other members of the family—the two daughters, Leonora

5

and Ruby.

The appearance of these two girls in this earthy family was anomalous. Leonora, the older sister, was like a water-lily in a pool of ooze and slime, delicately floating on the stagnant waters without a visible stain at a single point of contact. She had the Ellwell features, regular, angular, prominent; with her father's high forehead and finely tapering hands, and also her father's thin unwholesome skin. But instead of the livid tan complexion of the man who had beaten about the years of his life, the woman's pinkish transparency likened her again to the water-lily of the Middleton ponds. Her sister Ruby was more striking, much in the florid style of her brother. While she was young, she would be delicate enough to carry this kind of beauty; ten years might bring about an unpleasant fulness of bloom. Both had been petty invalids over many small ills, until now the monotony of the Four Corners was bringing about a gentle activity and health.

If the mother was will-less in the general concerns of life, she had shown one power in forming her daughters upon her own ideal of refinement. It was the way of life for men to be brutes, in a curious coarse fashion in speech, in appetites, in tastes; all that was an unaccountable arrangement of providence. So likewise it was befitting women to be chaste and refined, and to endure. Leonora comprehended her mother's sad position, yet she never held her father responsible. Men were made so, with a necessity for wickedness; some day she would be called upon to marry such a man, and suffer patiently, without scandal, a similar experience with vice. The woman's task was to keep fresh and unspotted herself, her home, her rooms, like some cool temple hidden away from summer heats and noisy commonness.

This girl of eighteen knew the family story as thoroughly as her mother; knew the disgraceful episodes, the unstable condition of fortune which they must expect. Tranquilly, daintily she trod her way, avoiding "scenes," covering up brutality, ignoring beastly talk or unpleasant dinner companions; occupying herself with her fresh dresses, or household matters; now decorating a room in the old Four Corners, or watering the ivies that were replacing the gnarled woodbines. Mrs. Ellwell had never kept improper books from her daughters —it seemed so hopeless—and she read what her father read, accepting the lurid picture of life presented in the novels plentifully scattered about the house as probably correct, yet with an indifference and weariness. Some cool twilight at the Four Corners, when the little tasks of the day had been done, before the carriage arrived from the station with the unaccountable male element of life, she might sit for a reflective half hour wondering why it had all been made so; why passion was recklessly rampant in life; why the world creaked in its action, groaning over the follies so thickly spread in its course.

In the daring of dreams, provoked by the long shadows and the deep quiet, other forms, strange possibilities, might flicker in her mind; but she was a woman! And soon it was time to dress for the long dinner.

There were evenings when the carriage returned empty, merely a telegram at the most, to account for the broker's absence; and these nights, sad for the neglected wife, were a relief to the daughter. The sweet monotonous day could go on (the country day she secretly loved when there were only women about the house) even down to night with rest, the shrieking world banished. There were other evenings when Ellwell drove up alone, morose, biting his iron-gray mustache in sullen disgust and ennui at some failure, perhaps in self-discontent and fear. Leonora met him at the veranda with a kiss, and a bubbling, clever greeting that dragged out a smile. Dinner was then a pleasant place for talk, the elder daughter taking the lead and holding it until she had roused the others. And there were other evenings when the broker brought with him friends, anyone he happened upon, when he was excited and loud, and the daughter had fears of the end. If the talk grew too boisterous, the women would hurry the courses and then withdraw to a side of the veranda, to sit sadly by themselves. If a quieter man, or some young fellow from Camberton, slipped away from the dining-room and joined them, they would talk gayly, simulating ease and naturalness.

For all this tolerance Mrs. Ellwell had the reputation with the broker and his companions, of being "a good woman" and a "good wife." And Ellwell considered that he had redeemed his note to propriety in marrying and having children, who become hampering things when a man is in a tight place. The servants gossiped, were insolent at times, but in such a household there were many pickings. The Middleton people, driving by at night within sound of the noise when the Four Corners was garishly lit, would repeat the family story and recall old Roper Ellwell, who lay in a green mound near his first church. But the broker, the "village magnate," as his daughters called him, was generous and free-handed in the parish. A "high liver" but "a good fellow" was his reputation; so it was considered a good thing for Middleton that the Ellwells had returned to the Four Corners.

From the serene frugal household of Roper Ellwell where the wife had fitted boys "in the classical tongues" for Camberton, the family had come to this uncertain state, feverish, like the fickle fluctuations of the stock market; now prodigal and easy, again in a panicky distress with dire fear of unknown depths of poverty and humiliation. Whatever happened—reckless, with a philosophy that did not embrace the morrow.

III

Roper second's set dined at Tony Lamb's in Camberton. For the most part they belonged to the same club, the A. Ω., and were congenial souls—young men, rich, from the great cities, who were taking the Camberton degree as a brevet in the social profession. In winter they could be found at the New York and the Boston hotels; in summer at the Bar Harbor hotels.

A few men of different stamp were left over from a previous college generation of A. Ω.'s, such as Jarvis Thornton, who had begun when a boy out of school to dine with his old schoolfellows at Tony Lamb's, and had kept it up from inertia and the loose liking of college fellowship, long after his way had parted from that of the present A. Ω.'s. Thornton had entered Camberton with all the distinction that a well-connected Massachusetts family, easy circumstances, and distinct scholarship would give. His course had been a gentle current of prosperity. He took first a high degree in the college, then a good degree in medicine. Now he was engaged in pushing forward some biological work on which he had already published a monograph and which had brought him membership in some learned societies.

One day at the beginning of the long vacation, Roper Ellwell and he found themselves alone at dinner. Young Ellwell was bored with the prospect of his own companionship for a lonely drive to the country.

"I say, Thornton," he threw out at random, "come down to our place over night. The cart will be round in a few minutes."

Thornton, flaccid from hot days in the laboratory, welcomed any proffered excuse for a loaf. So they jogged away in the soft evening, from the cropped green hedges and the red brick buildings of Camberton into the country turnpike, smoking and keeping a peaceful silence. After athletics and carts had been talked out there was not much to start fresh conversation with. Camberton slipped away, with its endless problems, its ambitious prods. Jarvis Thornton entered another atmosphere when the cart crunched the gravel of the drive at the Four Corners. The Ellwells were on the veranda. "Who are the Ellwells?" Thornton asked himself as he found a chair next the white dress of the daughter. "And why did I get myself into a family party for a day and two nights without knowing what to expect?"

He discovered an order of things he had never seen before in the rounds of his proper visiting list—the broker world. Ellwell had the possibilities of a gentleman, and in comparison with the three or four companions that he had with him this Sunday, his manners were distinguished. He was a Camberton man, he would have Jarvis Thornton understand, a classmate of Thornton's father, and if their paths had separated, Ellwell, nevertheless, had a position equal to the Thorntons. As for the others, they were clerks, who in one way or another had managed to get their seats—men with no great permanent stake in the community, the modern substitute for the condottiere class. The Four Corners gave them a place to eat and drink and play a long game of poker, which amusements satisfied their cravings for diversion. Jarvis Thornton was a mere young prig that had walked inadvertently their way; young Roper Ellwell joined the Sunday game, while Thornton was left with the women to pass the day. The Sunday went off quietly with a long drive in the afternoon. At dinner Thornton sat beside the elder daughter. There were stretches of silence, for the general talk and the table interested him more than his companion. The other men discussed business or scandal; old Ellwell told stories that were broad and fatuous, to which young Ellwell responded with heavy laughter. Ruby joked with an old-young man named Bradley, a broker, who had been winning in the day's game. As they came near the end of the long dinner Mrs. Ellwell excused herself. Thornton scrutinized his companion. The fumes of the place seemed to circulate about her unnoticed.

"Does she understand it?" Thornton asked himself. "Is this abstraction a mere bluff because I am a stranger? Or is she only bored?"

When she noticed that Thornton was not eating or drinking she questioned him mutely with her eyes.

"Shall we leave?"

He nodded. She rose and opened the long window—passed out, as if accustomed to avoid the puddles of life. She led the way to the farther end of the veranda, where only an occasional high voice could be heard. When she had settled herself on a lounge, she sighed inconsequently.

"But perhaps you didn't want to come? You can go back. We always walk about a good deal you know, and nobody will notice. You will want your coffee and cigar; and Colonel Sparks tells amusing wicked little stories. I will stay here, though."

"And I think I will," the young man added, simply. "It's really hot."

She opened her eyelids, which usually hung a little down as if heavy.

"It tired you too, did it? Somehow I never felt so weary from it as I do to-night."

"Is it always just so?" he asked, bluntly.

"Why, of course; why not? There are different people. But dinner is always the chief affair of the day in our house; you see the men are free then and their cares are over. My father is very particular about dinner, but it is tiresome sometimes."

Talk dropped. This line was dangerous.

"Tell me," she said again in curious inquiry; "you are not one of Roper's set?"

"No, he is some years my junior."

"But that does not make any difference. You never belonged to Roper's set. Isn't it very dull being a grind? Roper says you are a dig and fearfully clever."

"One must play for something." He waived aside the compliment.

"But how do you do it? Tell me just what you do every day."

Thornton was willing to take her seriously. He sketched his humdrum labors, the prizes in his way of life. "And it isn't so stupid," he ended with a laugh, "to play the game that way when once you have begun it." He added carelessly, as if to himself, "the body will give you only a few sensations, such a very few, and so humiliatingly inadequate."

"So *we* live for the body," the girl said, sharply, diving into his meaning.

"How do I know?" Thornton replied, irritated at his foolish remark.

"No you meant it; you meant it, and I suppose it is so. But one feels the body so constantly. Neuralgia racks me, and fatigue. Some days one would do anything to satisfy the cravings of that same body you seem to think we shouldn't pamper."

"If you give in you must do more another time," he added a little solemnly.

"How you must despise us!" Her eyes flashed suddenly. "You live coolly, tranquilly on for something at the end, never, never forgetting to have balance."

"Nonsense, I am blue at times, and life is tame."

"And we stumble about with our senses, making a muddle of our earth."

"Here is the carriage already!" It was a relief to find an excuse to break away.

"You will not come again, I fancy?" she asked, simply. An hour ago he would have answered yes, meaning in his heart never. Now the unsolved woman opposite prompted him to say: "If you want to see me again, if I may?"

"Come down some, some week-day, when it is so quiet. We can have more talk, and I promise you it will do you good to mix with the herd occasionally."

She laughed lightly.

"The blood has run out," Thornton mused, as the cart rolled on through the gentle night. "This fellow here is a flabby lump. She has neuralgia and long stretches of apathy, and other ills. Her children stand to lose, if she ever has any. She has kept the frame of the splendid old stock, but in its house the nerves and tissues are morbid and she is waiting," he paused, and then the words came, "waiting for dissolution and endless rest."

"Have another cigar?" His companion interrupted his musing.

"The old man keeps a good lot. Whew, how he plays! I left the little game; the family couldn't stand two in that. The old man will be savage this week. He can't play against that Bradley. Bradley is a regular sucker. I tipped the pater a pointer on that long ago, and got well cursed for my pains. When the old man gets on a tear there's no stopping him; no let up until he bucks his head against something hard. Well," he lashed the horse into a gentle gallop, "he can't kick at my batch of bills. When he gets on a high horse, I know how to fix him." He laughed. Jarvis Thornton turned a curious eye on his companion. Just this kind of intimacy in families he had never experienced—an armed neutrality of viciousness. He was anxious to get on, to reach his Camberton rooms, where the Sunday forlornness was peace after this swinish atmosphere. Once back in his arm-chair, in the familiar confusion of books and papers and letters lying about, he wondered again what curious freak had led him to accept Roper Ellwell's invitation. The Four Corners faded from his imagination into a murky blur, with one central point of white light made by a thin summer dress, a girlish figure, a face that had come into the world tired —devitalized.

The next morning he plunged again into a stress of work with his old swing and intensity, as if single-handed at one spurt he was to make his way to the close of his labors. He ate his hurried meals at a little restaurant near the laboratory, and came back to his rooms late at night, unexhausted, nervously eager to begin again.

IV

Ten days went by. One morning he woke late, listless and unprepared for the usual tussle. The June sun was pouring into his rooms, the old portières shaking gently in the soft breeze. Outside the world was flooded with sunlight. The new green grass, the full bushes along the paths, the warm blue of the sky seemed to mock his petty ardors, his foolish boyish designs of making prodigious strides. Life was not accomplished that way. One made a little, a very little step, then came lassitude; later, one must go over the same ground again. There were no great strides in nature. All was accomplished by subtle change. He dressed leisurely and looked about for a comfortable breakfast. There was something stronger than work in the world, especially to-day. He longed to meet the sunlight and earthly blessedness; it was such a small thing to fag one's self out at the laboratory. Half unconsciously he strolled toward the livery stable where he kept his nag. And then a quarter of an hour later he found himself on the turnpike, trotting along the fresh-water meadows, sniffing the air and the scented brooks. He laughed at himself. His horse plunged, freakish from his long rest in the stable. Suddenly he spurred on and rode furiously over the country roads, as if mad to reach a certain end. A little later, he cantered up the gravelled drive of the Four Corners, his horse wet and trembling, and he with a craving unexplained, a desire that had found a swift, brutal expression.

"You took a long time to think about it," she was looking up at him reproachfully, cool and fresh, with a morning blitheness about her, a physical calm that he had not felt before. The horse shivered and poked his head around to look at her.

He flung himself off the horse, and took her hands; she reached him two as if one for a handshake would be inexpressive.

"But it is splendid now that you have come! We have a whole, long, quiet day!" Her tones were calm and slow, full of the summer peace and warmth. He felt straightway content with himself. "Come," she continued, smiling. "I will make you a cool drink. Mamma has gone to town and Ruby is off somewhere in the pony cart." When she had left him on the veranda he laughed at his prudish fancies that had pestered him a fortnight ago. This June morning she had exactly the necessary amount of animation and health. All was well with her, and at peace.

They had much gentle desultory conversation. She took him about the place, showed him the old orchard where her great-grandmother's pupils had played

12

—one end was now made into a tennis-court, and the stable with its traces of the old barn where the Rev. Roper Ellwell had kept his horse and cow. Then there were little pigs and chickens, the various gardens that were all dear to her, where she patted and caressed the plants as if they had been alive. She took him to her own den, a little room where the grandfatherly sermons had once been written, and where hung a copy of that oil portrait which Thornton had seen in the Camberton Hall.

"Am I not like him?" she asked suddenly, placing herself in the same light as the portrait.

"Yes," Thornton answered, "with a difference."

"What is it?" she pressed him anxiously.

"I don't know, the something that has come in with the three generations," he answered, slowly.

"Tell me honestly," she persisted, with all the egotism of youth aroused over a personal verdict.

"Shall I?" he said, seriously. She grew grave, but nodded. Thornton watched the color leave and a trace of helplessness cross her face.

"The old fellow," he kept looking from the portrait to the woman before him, "in spite of his stiff board costume and the manner he's painted in, was a great lump of fire. It burned hard in him, burned away flesh and common passions; he must have been a restless, fervent man. You are calmer," he ended, stupidly.

"Yes, you mean that his fire has burnt out; that I am weak as water, when he was strong."

"No, not that, exactly," Thornton protested.

"Yes, you did," she reiterated, sadly. "And it is so, too. I am generally so tired. There are only hours like these, when something flows in and I forget things and am happy. But it fades away, it fades away."

They stood silent before the portrait. Suddenly she remembered herself.

"Luncheon must be ready."

Ruby came in for luncheon and made amusing talk. She had been into the village and was full of the farmers.

"I should think they would go crazy," she ended, scornfully. "What have they got to live for? I don't wonder that the girls go into the mills and do anything rather than sit about this little hole."

Later they set out for the fields as the afternoon sun was quietly going down behind the fringe of pines that skirted the horizon. The atmosphere of the day had changed and become like the still calm of perfected life. The little aspirations of the morning, the fascinations of nature, had given place to a content full of warmth. Miss Ellwell took a winding wood-road that led first across the meadow, then over the pine-needles to a little pond. As they sauntered along Thornton watched his companion draw in the saturated air of the summer afternoon, as if consciously living thereon. She seemed to him detached, like a plant that drew its best power away from man, in fields and woods, a kind of parasite.

"You love this?" he said, idly.

"Love it! I live on it. I come out here and sit down under the trees and close my eyes. Then the odor from the earth seems to enter me and make me over. Do you suppose grandfather Roper ever had such desires, such coarse joys in nature?"

"No, his ancestors had lived that for him. He had it stored up in him, and he gave it out in moral passion."

"And—they have gone on giving it out in passion——"

She raised her heavy lids questioningly, dreamily.

"So I must be planted again, for I am exhausted. Ah, well, she is a kindly mother, is old nature, and I like to lie down in her arms."

A little brook flowed sluggishly about big tufts of meadow-grass. The late violets and swamp pinks sent up heavy odors, mixed with a strong earthy smell. They seemed to be in the midst of nature's housekeeping and walked lightly as unannounced guests. They wandered on to an open patch in the woods and sat down, sinking into the dry, heated wood-moss. Thornton had no desire to talk; she, who had listened to him the other time, now took him in charge.

"You are so far away, here, in the heat and the earth; so far away from the world. One gets tired always trying to catch up, and always being tired."

As she talked he felt his limbs heavy in obedience to her words. His mind became tranquil as under the influence of a narcotic; it seemed such a little thing what he did over there in Camberton, and so far removed from the strong pulse that beat beneath his body deep down in the earth.

"Why are men so foolish," she whispered on. "We want really a few things only; quiet, rest, peace, tranquil bodies, and this great earth to shimmer and change forever." His eyes followed her face. Her skin was so transparent that each word seemed to make a dot of flashing color; her bosom gently moved in rhythm to her words, and her eyes with the heavy falling lids smiled at him in conspiracy with the mouth.

"But that is not all the story—repose!" his words sounded hollow, like a lesson he had learned by rote and propriety had obliged him to repeat.

"No!" her voice was lower yet than ever; "then comes love, and with love will flow in the passion and energy of life!"

The words moved her body. What she said seemed to him intensely true for the moment. Again propriety offered protest.

"And the other things—success and reputation and the good that the world needs."

She moved her hands carelessly.

"You would not need them." There was great scorn in that *them*. They lay quietly for several minutes while the earth murmured about. She had drawn him passively into her net. Like some parasitic growth she was taking her strength from him. But it was a new side to him, this yielding, and so in a few moments he remembered that hard, angular self that went about the week in his clothes. He jumped up.

"I must ride back."

She followed without protest. She seemed to swim beside him, happy in elemental, very simple thoughts, a thin color flushing over her face.

"We have been so happy. It has been such a long, full day. Will you ever come again?" They stood in the shadows on the lawn. He was minded to say, *no*, but as he took her hand the Ellwell carriage drove up the country road. After glancing at it she blanched. Ellwell got out of the carriage unsteadily, with his large handsome face flushed and distorted. He was half drunk, and in a great passion. Seizing the carriage whip in one hand and taking the bridle of the horse by the other, he lashed the trembling beast for some seconds. Mrs. Ellwell slipped out of the rear seat and half ran into the house. Bradley got out of the carriage slowly, with a sneer on his face, and nodded to Thornton. He smiled, as if to say: "Badly jagged, old fool."

"Go, there is Pete with your horse!" Miss Ellwell whispered. He was about to put his foot in the stirrup, and get away from the uncomfortable scene, when old Ellwell turned toward him.

"Don't let me scare you, young man," he said, with his regulation courtesy, the air of the old Ellwells. Thornton shook hands with him, noticing his bloodshot eyes, the puffy folds under the eyelids, the general bloat of an ill-regulated human animal. "Are you going before dinner?" Ellwell continued. Thornton murmured something about duties and engagements. Ellwell bowed and lifted his hat. Miss Ellwell advanced as if to say good-by, then stopped. Her face was sad. Thornton's horse wheeled impatiently. He grasped the saddle, and a moment later he was down the road out into the self-respecting fields and woods, where all had the sanctified peace of a starlight night.

"She did not like to ask me again, poor girl," he murmured.

V

Whether Jarvis Thornton would have yielded again of his own accord to the impulse to travel Four Corners-ward remained unsolved. He had on hand some experiments that he was undertaking for a paper which he had to deliver at the close of the month. His day of dissipation seemed to spur him on once more along the accustomed path, and only in the few lazy moments at the end of the day did his mind recur to the still meadows baked in the June sun, and to the woman who had tempted him into a dangerous world. One evening, when he was speculating luxuriously on that day of impulse, Roper Ellwell knocked at his door and entered.

Ellwell had never been there before. Jarvis Thornton had seen him from time to time at the A. Ω.; but a fast set, the Roper-Ellwell crowd, having made the club over into a drinking and poker-playing establishment, he had ceased to go there frequently. Ellwell was considerably battered, Thornton noticed, as he invited him, coolly, to take a seat and help himself to a cigar. He had come to pour himself out, and a dirty enough story there was to tell. He had been dropped from Camberton for general inadequacy; but that was the least of his troubles.

"I could go to the old man and tell him that," he explained, "his own record at Camberton wasn't any too fine, and he has a grudge against the old place. I am in here for a lot of money, which he will have to stand. But——"

Thornton looked at him unsympathetically, without commenting on his story. Why should he be troubled with the Ellwell excesses in the fourth generation? He failed yet to see the point to all these confidences.

"Your break-up is fairly complete," he said at last, coldly. "Many go down here, make a slip and bark their shins, but you have used two years in doing for yourself altogether."

Roper Ellwell hung his head.

"So the Dean said; and there's something else." Jarvis Thornton ceased to smoke as he went on. "I am married; the old man will never stand that, and it will break up the mater and my sisters fearfully." In short, he had come to Thornton, with the confidence that an acquaintance with an older man inspires, to beg him to break the news to his people. Imbeciles gravitate to the strong.

"Why don't you go yourself?" Thornton inquired, sick of the foolish affair. But one glance at the drooping, disjointed, miserable figure before him answered his question. He sat for some minutes debating the point with himself. He could make a conventional excuse, and play the man of the world, who did not involve himself with unpleasant people. But his imagination presented the picture of the two sad women; their last hope knocked away by this cropping out of the family blight. Perhaps he could put it to them in a better light than either Roper or his father. He saw again the girl's face standing on the lawn in the summer twilight—a face that must be constantly sad.

"Well," he said, "is she a bad lot, the woman you have induced to share your future?"

Young Ellwell was too miserable to take fire at this brutality.

"No, she isn't their sort though; she is a Swedish girl; she is a nurse in a hospital."

"You were forced to marry her?" the older man asked.

Ellwell nodded assent.

"And now she is making it uncomfortable for you."

"I am trying to find something to do," the young fellow protested. "Then I won't trouble them; but if I go down there the old man will fling me out of the house."

In short, Jarvis Thornton rose early the next morning, and before the sun had heated the road, was on his way to the Four Corners. There was not much that he could do, after all, in his pitiful errand; at least, for the mother. One more insult for her to accept, to be borne in stupid passivity. But for the daughter who had to live, it would be a different question; and by the time he had reached Middleton, he had not made up his mind how the tale was to be told.

It was warm when he walked his horse over the gravelled drive at the Four Corners. Mrs. Ellwell and her elder daughter were sitting on the piazza sewing. Pete was washing carriages; the dogs were asleep in the grass. The place was quiet and in peace. The women received him cordially; a bright color spread over the girl's face with a contented smile that seemed to speak intimately to him. He plunged into his business quickly, putting the case sympathetically before them. They listened without a word, the girl's face trembling and twitching slightly. Ruby had joined them, and Thornton interrupted his story, but Mrs. Ellwell motioned him to go ahead. While he was talking he hunted about for some bit of light to throw on the situation at the end. "He wants to go away, and it might be best, if we can find something for him. I have an uncle in Minnesota on a railroad. He might find a little place to transplant him to." He stopped.

18

"You have an uncle in Minnesota," Mrs. Ellwell repeated, mechanically, her dry eyes staring idealess at him. "You are very, very kind." She rose and walked into the house.

"Fool," Ruby muttered; her dark face flamed up angrily. Thornton noticed how much she resembled her handsome father. She had more fire in her than Roper second. "I suppose he hadn't pluck enough to come home with his own story. Father will be pretty mad. What did he *marry* that woman for!"

"Well," Thornton answered, calmly. "Perhaps we can build on that, the fact that he *did* marry her. That seems to me the most promising part of it."

The young girl cast a contemptuous glance at him and rustled into the house after her mother. Miss Ellwell had not uttered a word; her face was bent over her work; and he noticed a few suspicious spots on the dark linen cloth she was hemming. He turned his face away to the sunny lawn and the dark, full-leaved trees that lay beyond the road. A flock of sparrows were rowing in sharp tones among the leaves. The house-dog picked himself up lazily and walked over to Thornton, placing a wet muzzle on his trousers. The place was so peaceful, such a nest of an old Puritan! And here were the demons that the divine had warred against holding his home as their arsenal. When he permitted himself to turn his face to the girl at his side, she was grave and pale, and somehow exhausted. All the weariness of the struggle between flesh and will seated itself in her heavy-lidded, sad eyes.

"You must be a brave woman and help him," Thornton said, feeling the conventionality and silliness of any remark. "He mustn't be hounded out of here like a dog, but made to feel that he can make a decent future." She nodded. "It isn't the money," she said at last. "Though I can't see where it will come from. Nor the marriage, but the perpetual disgrace. It goes on increasing. We are all bad, worn out; dear old grandpapa was the last good one. It is what you call a curse, a disintegration. Why struggle? If we could all go to sleep and sleep it off? There is nothing ahead, nothing ahead!"

"That is folly," Thornton explained. "We have all been held in thrall by this curse of heredity. It has been talked at us, and written at us, and proved to us, until it makes us cowards!"

She looked at him sadly.

"'The sins of the fathers unto the third and fourth generation,'" she repeated.

"Damn!" He rose excitedly. "That is the most awful doctrine in the Bible, and we have believed it like sheep until we really make it true. When a weak man wants to go to thunder, he thinks of an uncle who was a drunkard, or a father who was a thief, and he goes and does likewise. Naturally! And now science comes along and says it isn't so, or at any rate there is strong doubt about it. In a few years we may prove that it isn't so and free mankind from that superstitious curse."

The girl comprehended him but half. "Why, I think that old grandfather Roper must have been a very passionate man, who fought against himself and conquered."

"Yes," Thornton admitted, "there was a lot of vice bottled up among the Puritan saints. It has been spilling out ever since, but that makes no difference," he went on vehemently to explain his theories. Somehow, now that his heart was touched, he put passion and conviction into what his sober reason held as speculation. He made clear to her the newest theories from Germany. He had come out as a diplomat in a distasteful cause; he became a pleader full of conviction. His imagination woke into a flame, and he saw anew, vitally, all the old problems that he had handled coldly in the laboratory. The woman sat dumbly, sucking in his statements and arguments. Then, as they stood on the grass waiting for Pete to bring up his nag, she said:

"We are free, you think." Her mind was laboring with his words.

"In a large measure, we can start fresh: the die is not cast beforehand." He added less warmly.

"But we copy what is about us. If we can't escape from what you call the current of ideals we are born in, what difference does it make? It amounts to the same thing!"

She, the woman, pleaded with him, the man, to free her, to take her away. He answered, tenderly:

"We can; each one can live his own life as a stranger to his shipmates. You have done so."

"It means a sacrifice. Some one must lift us. From some other life we could get the strength, and that other one loses—just so much as he gives."

Thornton's brows contracted. She read the comment of reason that ran beside his text.

"Who knows? Everything can't be weighed in scales."

She did not ask him if he would return; she knew in her heart that he would.

VI

Certain natural results followed from Jarvis Thornton's first interference in the Ellwell family troubles. He felt bound to do what he could with the Minnesota uncle to secure some kind of a berth for young Roper. In a few weeks he was able to make another journey to the Four Corners, with the definite offer of a small agency in a little frontier town. He found the family conditions troubled, but temporarily quiet. Old Ellwell, after a passionate and violent attack, had lapsed into a glum silence. The son kept out of his way; hung about the premises during the day-time, and took himself off as often as the mother and sisters could find money for him to spend. After several visits to the Four Corners, in such times of family stress, Thornton found himself on the most intimate terms with the young woman who seemed to realize the suffering most.

He made up his mind that, come what might, he should, in justice to his father, tell him the story. Thornton's father was an elderly man whom most good Boston people were glad to know. He had a little fortune; he owned a comfortable little brick box on Marlboro' Street; he had cultivated enough tastes to keep him reasonably occupied ever since his wife's sudden death years ago. Jarvis Thornton enjoyed his father, and the enjoyment was reciprocal. The two had put their heads together and planned out the younger man's life-work, and each felt an equal interest and responsibility for the success of their speculation. What the father's career had lacked in effectiveness, they now determined should be supplied by Jarvis. So the son felt already some compunctions when he realized how far he had gone in this important matter without putting his father in the way of criticizing it.

It was a stifling July evening that Jarvis took to open the matter to his father. The old man had been unusually silent, almost preoccupied during the dinner they had eaten together in the little back dining-room. The son noticed that the heat had told on his father, and he blamed himself for keeping him in this dusty, deserted town, while he completed his laboratory work. The electric cars made a great whirr, just around the corner, every few moments, and the little strip of park behind the house was full of the poor people who had crawled out of their hot holes to get some breathable air in the green spots abandoned by the rich. Jarvis Thornton cast his eyes lazily over the dusty library where they had gone for their smoke. Among its tall rows of sober-looking books he had got his first taste for the life he was beginning to lead, the life on the whole that seemed to him the most satisfactory of any he had looked at. There was a gulf between him and this passion-ridden mob which swarmed about the public parks in a hot summer; there was, also, a gulf between him and his neighbors in the contiguous brick boxes, who strove merely to make the boxes comfortable. And to his father who sat opposite to him, his fine thin face with the short gray beard occasionally lighted by the red coal of his cigar, he owed it all. Somehow to-night he felt that he was about to propose a raid across that gulf, a voluntary abandonment of the calm, effective position that he had been blessed with.

He had no difficulty in broaching the affair. To discuss a matter with his father was like talking to a more experienced and patient self.

"Did you ever know the Ellwells?" he began, simply. "One of them was the old pastor in the Second Church, and his grandson is on the stock board now." The older man nodded. Then he continued, describing his first introduction to the family, his impression of the Four Corners, his first visit there, with clear, simple portraits of the various Ellwells of this generation. When he came to the slump of Roper Ellwell, second, he found it less easy to explain how it had involved him. His last visits to the Four Corners he passed over hastily, and after a few broken remarks about the woman who had drawn him there, he came to an awkward silence. His father kept on smoking, as if waiting for a final statement. As it did not come, he spoke, in a clear, impartial voice.

"Yes, I have known all the Ellwells except these young people. I was just out of Camberton when the war broke out. John Ellwell shirked then; it was not much to do to go to the front. It was in the air to fight." He paused to let this aspect of the case sink in. "Later I was chairman of the committee that requested him to leave the Tremont Club. And still later, when his swindle on the exchange came to light, I helped his father hush the matter up. He was a bad lot."

"Yes," his son answered slowly. "An unusually bad lot. He is rotten!"

"Of course, besides the scandals we have mentioned there were, probably are, others with women. What you say about the children shows how impoverished is the blood. The son could hardly end otherwise. You have given him a new soil to grow in, but the end must be there!"

The old man pointed stiffly to the street. Jarvis Thornton made no reply. Presently his father continued:

"They were not transplanted in time. They are degenerate Puritans. There are a great many like them, who have petered out on the stony farms, or in little clerkships, or in asylums of one sort or another. The stock was too finely bred in and in, over and over, for three hundred years nearly. Insanity and vice have been hoarded and repressed and passed on." He seemed to speak with personal bitterness.

"We have the taint of scrofula, of drink, of insanity, all covered up. Those were wisest who scattered themselves forty years ago into new lands. Then the magnificent old stock took a new life. It would not be too much to say that wherever we find good life, hope, joy, or prosperity in our broad country, you may trace it all back to New England."

The son listened wonderingly to this essay on the Puritan stock.

"But I don't believe in it," the young man protested. "I don't believe that it is good science or good morals to hang about our necks this horrid millstone of heredity."

His father continued in his impartial tone. "You know how much of that rotten stuff is in our family. You remember the Sharps, and the Dingleys, and the Abraham Clarkes. You know your mother died from sheer exhaustion," the old man trembled, "and I have been spared for a fairly useless life by constant patching up. The war didn't knock me up only——"

"I will not believe it!" Jarvis Thornton uttered, in intense tones. His father sighed.

"And by some fortune you were spared; you have grown up strong and sound and equable. I led your interests to the line of work you have chosen, for a purpose——"

He paused again. "In order that sex, mere sex, might have no special unhealthy fascination for you; that you might meet these problems and treat them as judiciously as you would a matter of banking—without sentiment, without passion, without an ignorant, liquorish hallucination——"

The son raised his hand.

"And now it has come in a new way," he said, quietly, "through your pity and your generosity and your faith. But it has come."

What Jarvis Thornton replied was neither coherent nor weighty. He flung aside the idea of pity or generosity as absurd. He loved this woman for herself, because, because he loved her. His father smiled a sad, kind smile.

"The mother does not seem to have added much to the blood." He threw this out in order to get the subject back into more reasonable channels.

"No, she is a weak woman. But what of it? I don't marry the family. We shall leave them and build a new life, and break the curse." He smiled, slightly.

"Granting your beliefs that no harm would come to your children, that it is all chance about these matters," persisted the father, "still you *cannot* escape the family. You marry the conditions; they will remain with you. *They*, if nothing else, will ruin your life."

The younger man rose as if to shake off a physical bandage. For the first time in his life he felt conscious of a rebellion with the elemental conditions of existence.

"What if it does mean corruption and misery! I want my joy, my life, even if they write 'Failure' at the bottom of my page."

"No, no!" his father protested. "You will take the pain all right and the consequences like a man, but you will never believe that swinish statement you have just made."

This brought the younger man to his calmer mood.

"I hate them," he said, bitterly, "more than you can; but her I love."

"And to her you will sacrifice all?"

His father looked at him searchingly, longingly.

"Yes, if need be, *all*, but you!"

The old man smiled coolly.

"I shall not count long, and you are independent, anyway. But I don't care to put the matter on such a footing. We have not lived that way."

"I will do whatever you desire," the son said, "except——"

"I shall ask nothing," his father replied, gently. "If you mean to marry her you must do so now, when she will need you most. There can be no compromise, unless your own mind is divided."

As Jarvis Thornton left the house that night he felt that he had dealt his father a blow.

VII

Some days later when Jarvis Thornton took the familiar turnpike road he had not recovered from the serious mood his father's talk had brought about. It hung on him like a weight. He did not ride at a lover's pace; rather, cool and determined, with a spice of pride in following his own judgment. But the old man's prophecy met an answering fear in his own mind—it was dangerous to pluck roses from some ruins.

His father's sweetness in the matter got hold of him, and he began to appreciate, in a vague way, the yearning that old men have to witness fulfilment on the part of the younger generation. Mere age, he saw, reduces the complexity of desire, but renders it single and intense. Whether his father was right or not in his gloomy analysis, he was deeply convinced and foiled. His last method of success had turned out illusive, yet he had not reproached, nor domineered, nor dictated, nor appealed. He had expressed a little of his keen sorrow, but insidiously this attitude had tainted the young man's ecstasy.

Would *she* comprehend his father's nobility? He could hardly explain the situation to her in all its bearings, even if she were fitted to understand. And he felt that hers would be a woman's sympathy, so ready, yet on the surface. It needed a man, with his less expressive nature, to comprehend deep down the bearings of this case. However, if she loved him—it was pleasant to feel that she *did* love him—she must plan with him to defeat the old man's prophecy. They would cut loose from the conditions, come what might. He closed his mouth firmly. Manlike he planned as if he knew all the elements of the question.

His horse trotted up the little gravel way to the Four Corners. Suddenly she appeared standing on the big grooved millstone which served as a horse-block. Her white dress had an under bodice of pink, that gave her more than ever the appearance of an opening water-lily.

"I have a new walk for you to-day."

Her greeting betrayed no surprise. She was evidently sure of the outcome. As Thornton flung himself from his horse, he had a sensation of yielding—to the pre-arranged.

"But you must be so hot," she added, taking in his solemn face. "Come into the pantry while I make you a cocktail. Papa says I could get a place as a bar-maid."

With a ripple of contented laughter she led the way to the little pantry over the wine-cellar. It was stocked and arranged like a miniature bar; a high side-board was carefully crowded with polished cut-glass, and the little room exhaled aromatic odors from the various wines and bitters. He sat down near the open window while she busied herself in crushing ice to a flaky coolness and gathering the materials. To see her at this job seemed to put all of the solemnity of the occasion far away. Yet he sneered at himself for his prudery.

The sun blazed down outside on the scorched lawn; here the summer heat brought out all the pungent odors of the place, permeated, so it seemed, by the stock-broker, by the kind of American who could endure life only when his nerves were soothed in some way. Pfa! The atmosphere of the Four Corners' swine! They reminded him of the bondage to the flesh that in his masterful mood he hated. He sipped his cocktail and lit a cigarette, inhaling it with deliberation, noting with idle curiosity how his pulses responded by sharp little beats.

The escape from reality! He had always liked blunt reality, and believed in it professionally. You must have a sane mind and a normal body to believe in reality, and hence few cared for that kind of bitter bread. The mob tried to escape. Would he too, perhaps, try to escape? What a time he was losing from that slow methodical task he had set himself? Three months ago had occurred the first break in his regular current of thought, and now he was drifting about aimlessly in a mess of passions and desires.

"Do you like it?" Miss Ellwell asked, anxiously. He had it on his lips to say:

"I hate it." That would sound silly and incomprehensible, like an impromptu lecture on the sins of strong drink. His eyes wandered over her, resting on one white arm that lolled across the side-board.

"I like you," his eyes said. A wave of brutal indifference to everything but immediate desire surged in the man. However, tossing away his cigarette, he nodded.

A little dash of pink in her face and neck answered his eyes.

"Now come." She put back the last glass and pulled down the shade, shutting in the heavy odors.

They sauntered out through the orchard to the wood-road that led eastward from the Four Corners.

There was a section of Middleton dominated by a high hill, with a country pond at its foot, that possessed an air of distinction, of being apart from the flat village and the small barren farms. High stone-walls ribbed its green surfaces, meeting in a heap at the top, where also a few wind-blown apple-trees maintained their stunted growth. A little below the crown of the hill

26

there was a thick cluster of nut-trees. From this height one could see the Hampton hills to the east, outlined by a thin row of trees drawn as if with a heavy brush along the margin of the landscape. Elsewhere the hills were rounded bare mounds. Farther north this undulating line dipped into a green plain, and there, so the tradition ran, you could see on a clear day the white sails of coasting schooners and a shimmer of eastern light that might be the marshes of Essex, or indeed the blue sea itself. This apple-tree crowned peak was a kind of lookout from the dead country to the living sea.

Miss Ellwell brought Thornton out at the mound of stones on the crest; they rested their arms on the wall, looking east searchingly for the bit of blue coast and the sails.

"There, there, I can see it," she cried. He looked at her incredulously. There was nothing but a nebulous mass of blue. "Well, I have seen it," she protested, "two or three times. To-day it is a bit hazy."

"Why do you want to see it?" he asked, idly.

"Oh, it is so different! It is big and strange and unfamiliar; don't you like it?"

"'There is a world beyond!'" He answered without direct appositeness. They turned to the shade of the nut-trees. In the July sun the woods seemed asleep, merely soothed by a wandering breeze, and they flung themselves down on the warm ground. All about the air swam with pleasant, heated, drowsy, earthy odors.

As she took off her hat and nestled back into the undergrowth, Thornton felt her anæmic body, pale from the fatigue of the hot walk, as if the water-lily were drooping in the mid-day sun. Yet she was somehow intimately connected with the brooding earth. There were two bodies—the body of flesh that had come with fatigue and feebleness into the world, and the body of passion that was blooming into power.

She talked of the thousand trivialities that go to make the conversation between a man and a woman. Thornton lay silently, stretched on the warm leaves at her feet, feeling her bloodless face with its sharp blue veining. Each was conscious of a dynamic something in the air; their minds had a frank understanding while the talk skipped in and out among nothings. When she began once more to talk of the sea that lay down there beyond the green meadows and the blue haze, a faint rose-color of animation darted over the pallor and made the moist eyes flash. The sea! That stood in her mind for the mysteries of change, of the unknown. Thornton knew that this wistfulness after change had nothing definite in it, was merely a girl's hunger for motion; yet that had divided her in his mind from her kind.

"There is a world beyond," she murmured, in wondering repetition of his words. The branches of the nut-trees swayed in the odorous wind as if whispering, "Yes, yes, we know of it. That world beyond ... over the hills of flesh, and the tedious wastes of tired bodies, there *is* a world of peace beyond!"

Her eyes came to his face wistfully. He held the keys of that beyond.... Something had snapped in his well-ordered mechanism, and he was going, going, drifting will-lessly into feeling and longing. And the next moment he held her, looking into a face that burned with love. There were no words. Life had been too strong for his little plans; it had mocked him and driven him passionward, like a bit of straw caught in a gale. The hours swam on unheeded, while they rested there face to face. Then came the going home across the afternoon woods; she silent and content, he trying to account for himself. When he had speculated about such matters, he had seen himself discussing, quite properly, the serious affairs of life with some tall girl of distinguished carriage, some one of the many young women whose acquaintance had made up his Boston parties. He had expected that their conversation would grow more serious as this intimacy deepened, and that at last, having found themselves of one accord on the sober ideals of life, he should broach to her this final proposition involving both their lives. He had half imagined such a situation with several fine young women; the scene had always been played out in a drawing-room filled with bric-à-brac and heavy hangings, he in his long black afternoon coat. There had been a touch of solemnity in it, a weighty sense of responsibility that would have made their first kiss a little sepulchral.

Now, this! Her hand touched his; his mind left these bizarre images, and suddenly it seemed that life was one wilderness of woods in the late afternoon sun, down which he was fated to wander in a lethargic dream. One dominant feeling of tenderness; one indifference to the baying of reason—merely love, and the soft, warm earth, and the greenness of living things, and the woman whose dress brushed his arm. Ah! that was sweet and precious at any price.

VIII

He had put something in motion on that languid July day, and suddenly he was whirled along in a stream of consequences. There was an interview with Mr. Ellwell, a sudden opening of the Ellwell family arms, and he was one of them—not much to his relish. Ruby Ellwell brought out her engagement to Bradley, the young stock broker her father had chummed with. The Four Corners renewed its worldly life in a garden-party, at which both engagements were announced. Thornton had to stand in line with his new brother-in-law, and for all this disagreeable business, the sole consolation was the happiness the woman he loved found in it. For her it was a rehabilitation of the family, the first dawn of those better times she had looked for all these years.

He remembered for all his lifetime how his father had met her; how he had walked across the lawn, old, and gray, and aloof, and had taken both her hands. He had smiled at her tenderly, as if she were a little girl, much as he had smiled years before at Jarvis's mother. Then he had kissed her on both cheeks, and had stood patting her hands in a gentle caress. Later he had slipped away in the same quiet abstracted manner. For the rest of the day Jarvis Thornton had been a little sad, as well as bored, without knowing exactly why.

They had planned a simple wedding for September; they would walk to the village church, the old white box of a meeting-house where the first Roper Ellwell had led his congregation. Martinson, Thornton's youthful hero at the Camberton Theological School, would meet them in his episcopal robes on the little green in front of the church, and then the party, not more than a dozen, could walk together into the bare old building, and in the solemn quiet of the country noon complete the marriage. A quiet dinner, and then away from the Four Corners.

But it could not be so. The handsome Ruby wished to have a "function," some of the conventional excitements of this entertainment. The two sisters must be married together; a special train must come from Boston; a grand reunion would be held of all the old family friends who had shaken their heads over the Ellwell misfortunes. So the two quieter souls yielded, and the marriage left a bad taste in the young bridegroom's cup of joy.

Almost at once they had gone abroad to Berlin, where Thornton proposed to work for an indefinite time. It seemed to him that he should accomplish more than one object, by carrying on his work in Europe; he could insensibly divide himself and his wife from the Ellwell connection. All went sweetly for his first months; he had begun to regard his marriage as an idyl slipped in between pages of prose. But when their child was coming, his wife grew restless; she must go home, he saw; it was natural that she should long to return to her mother at such a time.

So back to Boston they had gone, Thornton contenting himself with the reflection that he could go ahead in Boston almost as well as in Europe; that fortunately he was not tied by money wants, and that the Camberton laboratories were always open to him. When the little daughter came he schemed a new move; he was offered a headship of a laboratory somewhere in the middle West. He began to feel the force of his father's remarks about transplanting.

Yet they never went. Another man got the appointment while he was persuading his wife. Her mother was so lonely, now that Ruby was living in New York. They had no necessity to live far away in order to earn money. When he proposed moving to Washington, the same ground had to be gone over again, and the same gentle obstinate resistance to be met.

"Go to Washington," old Thornton said when his son stood by his bedside during the last illness. "Go to Washington," he repeated, querulously. And as the younger man made no reply, but sat with his hands shoved in his pockets, brooding, the sick man spoke again, "You will never do anything here."

"Yes, we must make a move," assented his son in a voice that said "no."

After his father's death, they went to live in the Marlboro' Street house. There was no more talk of moving away. The Ellwells came in town for the winter, living in a flat at one of the new hotels near by. Mrs. Thornton had the habit of spending her mornings in the flat with her mother and the baby. Thornton could find no reasonable grounds for the rebellion he felt over this tie, this close proximity to decay in which he was compelled to live. Yet he loathed the thought that his child, unimportant as she was now, should begin her life by imbibing such a forlorn atmosphere.

He could tell each day what had been going on in those long morning hours; how his wife's sympathies had been on the rack; how mother and daughter had sighed over the unaccountable miseries of life. She seemed to him to come home with the old anæmic look, with the old restless hunger in her face, and then he was reminded that their child was more than delicate. It would lead him to envy mere gross flesh and blood, the coarse fibre of some riotously healthy common folk. Indeed it was a crime against his fellow-men, this maintaining a bankrupt stock unless he could patch it into vigor. There were hints too that fell indefinably now and then about the Ellwell affairs, the stock-broker's poor health, the perpetual disappointments that discouraged him. His wife had relapsed into the Four Corner's habit of regarding incapacity and folly as mere misfortune. It irritated him to realize all this sentimental pity over a blackguard. Yet she was right; she had the opinion of centuries on her side; was she not their daughter before she was his wife?

There were times when Ruby came on from New York for a visit, bringing her child, a boy, with her. Thornton grimly noted this vigorous little animal of a nephew and compared him minutely with his own feeble child. He compared also the mothers. Ruby had already begun the period of over-bloom. The Bradleys, he gathered, lived a kind of a tramp existence, moving from boarding-house to hotel as Bradley went up or down. And Ruby, with all her assurance and her affluent person, had not lost the Ellwell ailments. Yet to her child had been given the strong stock he envied. Nature had coolly overlooked his, and carried her blessings where they were notdeserved.

Such reflections made him more tender to his wife. He wondered if she ever thought of this contrast.

When he was working in his little back-room study, he wondered what the two sisters could find to talk about for hours. He fancied that they were going over the old items of the family budget, the thousand trivialities of family gossip that never seemed to be ended and never lost their interest. One day he could hear Ruby earnestly talking—she had just come from New York—and then he thought he caught the sound of suppressed tears. After a time he rose nervously and walked out to his wife's room where the sisters were.

Ruby's face was excited though sullen. She had not taken off her hat, and in her haste her gloves had fallen on the floor by the door. Her sister was crying, quietly. "What's up?" Thornton turned sharply to Ruby, his voice betraying his desire to sweep her out of his life forever.

A slight sneer crossed her face. She said nothing, and punched the footstool with the toe of her boot sullenly, as if resenting his appearance. As Thornton waited for an explanation, she rose and picked up her gloves.

"You'll have to tell him," she spoke roughly to her sister. "I'm going over to mother's."

Thornton accompanied her to the door. Her air was defiant and sullen; Thornton contemptuously refrained from questioning her.

"Well," he said, quietly, when he had returned. Something very bad was to come; it had been hanging about in the air for months.

"Jarvis, I can't tell you; it's so awful. What shall we do? Poor Aunt Mary and Aunt Sophie!"

"They have lost their money."

She nodded.

"Through Bradley?"

"Oh, Jarvis, I have brought you so much trouble; I am afraid I ought not to have kept you here in Boston."

"I don't see how that could affect this," he replied kindly to her irrelevant contrition. "Has it all gone?"

"I suppose so."

"How did he get hold of it?"

"I don't remember anything. Papa had it—all their money—to invest, and he let Ruby's husband have it to put in wheat. It's all gone."

Thornton had heard that John Ellwell's sisters had been left a small fortune by their father with strict directions to keep it out of their brother's hands. They were two delicate maiden ladies, who had floated about Europe aimlessly for a number of years, living in one watering-place after another. Their refusal to have anything to do with their brother had been one fruitful topic of family discussion. A few years before, however, when American stocks were booming, the two maiden ladies had withdrawn their hundred thousand from the woollen mill where old Mr. Ellwell had placed it, and had given it to the stock-broker for reinvestment. Their brother had always fascinated them. He was clever, wicked perhaps, but so clever that he always got into good things. The conclusion came shortly. For the last six months Ellwell had managed to keep up the interest; now he had come to the end of his rope, and he was about to commit suicide by selling his seat in order to provide a pittance, at least, for his sisters.

Husband and wife sat silent for a long time.

"Why did Ruby come to break the news?" Thornton asked at last. His wife looked at him timidly, then flushed.

"I suppose she thought we could do something; but what shall we do? We never have anything left over."

The bolt had fallen; Thornton traced its course in a few little moments.

"There is but one thing," he said, gently; "we must see that your aunts do not starve, at least for the present."

"You'll have to give up your investigations and laboratory work, and all that?"

She was striving to comprehend his situation, an effort that he had planned for her that July day when they had become engaged.

"For the present."

"How can you love me? Your life would have been so different. You have always said that you were equipped with ideal conditions, just enough money to work as you liked. And now you can't escape unless I die."

He disliked to utter commonplace lies; although she spoke the truth in her sudden realization of the facts to have him deny it, he could not protest; so he kissed her instead and said, later:

"We can't reckon things that way." Her old look of misery came back.

"You can't win with me."

"But I have won love."

And she was appeased.

From that date he had become a man in the sordid sense of the word. He had taken his father-in-law sternly in hand, presented the case firmly, and showed him the extent of the sacrifice his worthless life had made necessary. He paid from that day the normal income to the Misses Ellwell's bankers, but he gave the stock-broker to understand that was the end. Any further protection for him was not to be found in this life.

A few months later he hung out his shingle as practising physician and surgeon. There would be need enough of money in his life; the way to get it was by using his acquaintances in Boston and practising only about a few streets of the Back Bay. So at thirty he had begun the ordinary routine of a well-connected physician—the profession he had sneered at in his youth, the profession of polite humbug.

IX

The next fifteen years that carried Jarvis Thornton over from one generation to another passed with placid monotony. He had been decidedly successful. His little round of Boston streets where he doled out mental and physical encouragement, resounded with his praises. Moreover he was known as a "good fellow," an epithet that his warmest friends in Camberton days would not have bestowed on him. He was sleek and solid; well-groomed and rounded, in spite of constant activity, and if his scientific reputation was not more than mediocre, it was enough to give him a lectureship on neurosis in the Camberton Medical School—that necessary mark of approval for a doctor practising in his circle. He spent eight months of each year in Boston; the other four he practised at Wolf Head, a fashionable sea-side place that he had done much to promote. There he had built a roomy cottage on a little point of land, and he had shrewdly invested in the Improvement Company that held the best lots along the shore. He was a comfortable family physician to have about, with a good digestion and a desirable connection; in his few hours of recreation he could be counted on for tennis or yachting or a dinner-party, even with a dance attached.

One step that marked the prosperity of the Thorntons was their new house on Beacon Street, selected with much care in the short block or two of stable neighborhood. When they had moved into this new house, Mrs. Thornton had referred to the past indirectly.

"Why don't you take the sewing-room?"

"What for? I can't entertain patients on the third floor."

"You could use it for a laboratory for your things," Mrs. Thornton suggested vaguely. "I could get along without it."

The doctor smiled.

"Oh, I don't need so much room for that; I haven't over much time these days."

It touched him that she remembered, even remotely, the bearing of that tragic day when her sister had come to announce the Bradley rascality. Soon she began again, this time nearer the heart of the matter.

"Jarvis, you don't mind it so very much, the change you had to make, *now*."

"Now that I have more practice than I can attend to?"

The doctor's voice had an inexplicable tone in it at times which made his wife shy of intimate conversation.

"You are such a success," she struggled on; "and everything has come out so —peacefully."

"There are two verbs, my dear, which most people confuse: to succeed and to win." Then, as he noted her troubled face, he kissed her. "That bell has been ringing for half an hour. That is an outward and visible sign of the first verb. I must heed it."

When he left her, she mused over his words. Except for occasional disturbing moments like these, it never occurred to her that her dreams made in that hot summer at the Four Corners had not come true for them both. She had dreamed vaguely and she had realized vaguely. When she contrasted her husband's career with her father's, or with any other that made up the *répertoire* among her acquaintances, it seemed fair and unblemished. But men were exacting creatures, who rarely knew what was best for them, and who kept about them a fund of discontent to feed upon.

There was her poor father. He had given up now; Doctor Thornton saw that his wife's parents did not starve. Ellwell was a melancholy skeleton to meet on the streets, bent, walking stiffly at all his joints, his fleshy cheeks fallen in as if after a severe fever. He was shabby, too, though the allowance was a liberal one. Fine mornings he would crawl down Tremont Street to one of the hotels, and lounge away some hours in the bar-room, on the chance of meeting an old acquaintance. Frequently the doctor would hear his husky cough in the hall outside his office door, but the old man slunk away sullenly whenever the door opened. Thornton suspected that on such occasions drains were made upon his wife's allowance. Where else did it go to? He was minded at times to mention this degrading beggary, but always refrained. He would have to build his wife's character over from the foundations in order to make her appreciate his disgust, and he was not sure that he desired such an essential change in her, at least, now. She would confuse the issue: he would seem to be rebuking her pity and natural tenderness. So it mattered little if the old wreck wasted a few hundreds more on the pleasures he was capable of getting.

The doctor's wife had wavered between invalidism and delicate health for some years, and had settled into retirement until her daughter brought her out once more, first at Wolf Head, then in Beacon Street. The household, in spite of the fact that there were only three members, was known as an expensive establishment. But the doctor was supposed to be well off, and his practice was good for more than he spent. If he worked hard all the winter, he was not idle in the vacation months; his fawn-colored horse could be seen jogging about for miles up and down the coast. It was generally well into the evening before his dark face and burning cigar were seen on the path of the cottage.

The summer when his daughter was seventeen, had been particularly busy. They had had a stream of guests as usual, staying for a week or a fortnight, and the busy doctor had not paid much attention whether Ruby Bradley with her young son had come or gone, or whether the second cousins had yet arrived. The house was generally full. He liked that, although he chose to dine alone, quite frequently. His daughter, whom he had watched shrewdly, demanded people, and the safer plan, he thought, was in multitudes. She was a restless young person, tall like him, with fair skin like her mother, dark hair, and nervous, active arms.

"She will always have some man on hand to exercise her egotism on," the doctor reflected, impartially. So he fed her young men. The father and daughter went about a good deal together, and people made pleasant remarks over their intimacy. This summer the doctor thought about her on his long drives, and scrutinized the young men who lounged about his veranda. Most of them were boys in the calf stage, college youths, who were spoiling with vacation. These the doctor called the puppies, and treated indulgently. There were others who came to the hotel for short fortnights, impecunious young business men or lawyers who were looking about for suitable assistance in life. Such candidates were submitted to a close scrutiny, but nothing to warrant active measures had yet occurred.

He had made up his mind precisely about his future son-in-law. For two years he had studied his daughter, and nothing could shake his conviction that he had found the only safe conclusion to a difficult problem—a certain kind of husband. He must be rich, for Maud had inherited the Ellwell dependence upon luxury. And he must be able to devote himself pretty steadily to her whims, subordinate himself good-naturedly, and obtain for her whatever she might fancy for the time.

"She will want to express herself badly," was the doctor's comment. "If they should try to express themselves both at the same time, there would be explosions—rows and divorce and scandal—unhappy children." Once he said to his wife, forlornly, "She is too clever, poor child. She has been talking to me like a marchioness of forty for the last half hour. If this keeps on I shall have to domesticate her great aunts in order to have some children about the house."

The desirable husband must be able to place her well socially, for she had already shown herself keen in making distinctions. It gave her father a wicked pleasure to see her snub young Roper Bradley when he came with his mother to make their annual summer visit. She never mentioned her uncle Roper, and she extended compassion to the doctor on the subject of her grandfather

Ellwell.

The doctor was fond of her in spite of his analysis. He thought with pride that she was thoroughbred, capable of masterly strokes. Yet, alas! the opportunities for masterly strokes would come so rarely; meanwhile she was a dangerous, febrile, nervous, chemical compound—something to be isolated. With her five-day enthusiasms, her quick wit, her restlessness, her sense of dress, she would be fascinating.

"If she will only fascinate the right sort!" the doctor prayed. He smiled savagely at the picture he drew of the right sort, which, it is needless to add, was not a congenial type.

"An acquiescent fool for a son-in-law, a kind of gentlemanly valet!" And, "That, I trust, will be the end. Maud as a mother would be atrocious."

His daughter gave the doctor a certain kind of scientific interest. She harked back, so to speak, to former generations, perverting their simple instincts. Her devotion to the Salvation Army for one winter, he pointed out to his wife, was a recrudescence of the old Puritan pastor in his revivalist days. This manifestation would not be permanent, for there were so many other desires crowding each other in her brain. Just now she had developed a longing for art. The doctor had been obliged to exert himself to prevent her sudden departure for Paris, where she pictured herself living on two francs a day at the top of a very dirty flight of stairs.

"Perhaps she will elope," the doctor said to his wife, humorously. "But she won't elope with a mere man: she will go off with an idea and then come around to the front door to be taken back."

"I don't think she is very considerate," Mrs. Thornton hinted. Maud treated her at times with toleration. The doctor understood what that meant—her lack of sympathy with her mother's clinging to her family; deluging the Thornton house with Ellwells and their affairs.

"If she would only cultivate some serious interests, yours, and take the place of a son," thus Mrs. Thornton referred to her husband's youth and its sacrifices.

"I haven't any use for women doctors," Thornton replied; "and Maud as a nurse scrubbing floors would be more absurd than Maud in an Army Rescue Post."

For the art fever, however, the doctor felt to some extent responsible. He had allowed young Addington Long a certain right of way in the house. Long was the son of an old friend, a Camberton man, who had wrecked himself early in his career. Doctor Thornton had taken the boy out of his squalid home, sent him to a boarding-school, and then, as he promised well, paid his way at Camberton. The young fellow had not done anything remarkable, merely grown into a nice gentlemanly manhood, with a taste for illustrating, by which he picked up a few dollars for spending-money, and placed himself pleasantly in Camberton circles. When he graduated, Dr. Thornton fell in with his suggestions that he should like to try his fortunes as an artist. So Long had spent several years in a studio at Paris, and had done solid work. The doctor had felt encouraged with his experiment and treated him liberally.

This was only one of a number of similar experiments in young life that the doctor carried on silently. Earlier in life than most men, he had had the yearning to see others go where fate had forbidden him. A number of young doctors, studying in Berlin or Vienna, and some young scientists scattered over the country owed their freedom to his liberality. He selected his material here and there, without much apparent discrimination, but one test existed, known only to the doctor, a test that was strangely sentimental, and yet shrewd.

Long's interests had been outside his field, but the tenderness he had felt for the father caused him to make this exception. He had not made a mistake, however. Long had exhibited at Berlin and Munich, and had begun to sell his work a little. He was already spoken of by the international press as a promising young American artist. This summer he was at home, sketching in a village not far away, and the end of the day found him quite frequently at the doctor's dinner-table.

The doctor liked him. He had bought Long's first picture in the Salon and had procured him patrons. He took him off on his yacht whenever he had a chance, and the more he saw of the young man the more he was ready to bet on his future. "There is so much that is clean and wholesome in him," he observed to his wife. "He has managed to live over there without catching their cheap bohemianism." Mrs. Thornton felt at liberty to encourage Addington Long's intimacy at the house. But he would not do for a son-in-law; there would be two tragedies instead of one. So when Mrs. Thornton suggested that he should be asked for a visit during September, the doctor put the question off with irrelevant excuses; they had had too many people; September was his time for a rest; young Long should be getting down to hard work, not loafing in a comfortable cottage.

One evening toward the middle of the summer the doctor came home later than usual, and, wearied with his day's driving, he got out of his carriage and let himself into his grounds by the shore path. The evening wind was puffing casually across the bay; in the cottage above the lamps were being lit. The doctor walked slowly, thoughtfully, picking his way in and out of the shrubbery, thinking vaguely of the day's work, the cases visited, the cases to be visited on the morrow, the routine he had established. As his eyes rested on the cottage nestled in its little domain that commanded several miles of the shore-line, he reflected complacently on his business sense which had led him to develop Wolf Head. He had managed, so far, skilfully, and this matter of a daughter that would come to a crisis during the next five years should be handled successfully. No one could be said to have the confidence of the doctor; one would not look to him for confidences of any sort. Did he ever betray any doubts as to the desirability of his career? Indeed, he never put the question to himself. Fate had caught him in a vice; he had spent eighteen active years in padding that vice. Yet he mused as a man will at the close of a busy day, wondering what compelling power drives him over the wonted round.

Suddenly he heard voices on his lawn, and instinctively stepped from the gravel path to the grass. There was a long murmur of a low voice; he wondered at his own intensity in listening. Something in the timbre of the voice, some suppressed emotional quality, struck his experienced ear. When the sound ceased he advanced carefully along the hedge until he came to an opening that gave a view to the lawn. The voice was his daughter's, as he had guessed; beside her was stretched a man's figure in flannels, probably Long's. It was simple enough: tired after their tennis they had flung themselves down where the hedge sheltered them from the evening breeze and were talking. But their attitude arrested him; he felt an undue strain in the air. Presently Long spoke with a low, slow utterance, as if ordering his words. His face was turned away from the doctor, looking up steadily at the girl.

"Yes," he said, and the doctor felt he ought to walk on, "it's hard on a man. You see so many fellows who have failed who are just as good as you are ——"

"No, no; not just as good," the girl interrupted, "there is *something* different."

"Well, as far as you can see they are just as good; they have worked terribly hard. Then you shut your teeth and go in again, working desperately from the first light to the last peep until you are plugged out."

"Then?" his companion said, eagerly.

"Perhaps you crawl out to Lavenue's and sit there in the evening watching the people sip and talk, the girls sauntering home, or the students who are gassing forever. It doesn't seem to make any difference what you do then, whether you go on a loaf for a month and fool with those who play, or go home to bed and back to work in the morning. You think the idea will come some day whenever it gets ready, and that there is precious little use in slaving away on a one franc fifty déjeuner."

"Don't you think of home, America, and us who are anxious for you?"

"It seems so far away; and do you care unless I make a strike?"

The girl was silent; her face was turned away while she played with his answer.

"You know we do," shielding herself with a neutral plural.

"There's the other side," the young man's voice sounded out more buoyantly.

"You go around to some friends' studio and see what they are up to, and get ideas and go home with more spirit; or something good comes along, a picture is accepted, an order comes in. You think you have got there all right and it's only the question of a little patience. There's a good dinner or a little trip in the country—it's fine around Paris you know. Then I think of coming home with some kind of a rep., and how all of you will be glad—*you* at any rate, Miss Thornton?"

The doctor sighed and crept away.

"The condition for the fever," he muttered.

X

When he had entered his study he sat down to think. His man announced a patient, but the doctor made no reply. Suddenly he glanced up at the waiting servant.

"Will you tell Mr. Long as he leaves that I wish to speak to him."

Then he went on thinking. Soon there was a knock, and Long came into his study. The doctor motioned to the chair he had just left, and, reaching for a box of cigars, took one and lit it. Long watched him expectantly.

"Shall you stay on here much longer?" the doctor asked at last, in his usual composed manner.

"Oh, I don't much know. I want to get back to Paris in the winter if——"

"Don't bother about that," the doctor interrupted him, hastily. "You can trust me to find the amount, you know, until you are squarely on your feet; only," his voice grew sharper, "you won't do much here. You should go at once."

The young man stared.

"Sail next week," the doctor continued, blandly, but fixing his eyes steadily on Long's face.

"I don't know that I can accept——"

The older man waved his hand hastily.

"You can from me. I have been your father for a good many years."

There was a pause. Then Long blushed slowly. "I don't know that I can," he said at length. "Why are you so anxious to get rid of me?" It was the doctor's turn for silence.

"If you don't go now, you will not be likely to go for a long time." His eyes kept firmly on the young man's face.

"And if I have a reason to stay here?"

"There can be no reason stronger than your success."

"But there is—at least," he paused, awkwardly—"I feel there is, I hope there is."

"Do you know why I have backed you so persistently?"

"You have been awfully kind!"

41

"It was not altogether on your father's account," the doctor interrupted him. "I might have put you in some business and left you to fight your own way. That kind of experience we all know makes men, the successful men, who are tried and found capable of bearing strains. I have saved you so far from that struggle. Why?

"Because," continued the doctor authoritatively, "there are some men who care more to do some one thing, who love one object, more than they care for success, for fame, for pleasure. If they are defeated, if they never have the chance to do that one thing—perhaps the world is no poorer—there are plenty to take their places, but they are capable of misery, real misery, such as no common failure ever brings to the common man. They may be foolish; they may be idle and be drawn aside and think they are happier in doing what comes along, but that is never true. They are wretched. Such men can never love, except as an interlude. Do you understand me?"

The doctor paused at this sharp interrogation; Long's eyes had followed him wonderingly during his long monologue.

"So you thought——" he stammered.

"That you were made in that way," nodded the doctor; "an undomesticated animal."

Long sat brooding over this idea. The doctor went on in his low, swift tones.

"You have the hunger and the thirst for that work over there. You would play with a woman and then put her out of your heart into the street, or try to tame yourself. Which would be worse."

"And if I am not so sure that I am built like that? Suppose I am willing to make the sacrifice, if you call it that?"

The doctor's tone became neutral again.

"You refer to a possible interest in my daughter."

Long's face slowly flushed under the word "possible."

"Yes! at least, perhaps—I have never put it to myself exactly—indeed why do you ask?"

"May I ask how far that interest has gone?"

The younger man half rose from his chair.

"If it had *gone* at all," he said, hotly, "you would have known it."

"Yes," the doctor knitted his eyebrows, "that's all right. Don't feel disturbed. If I didn't consider you to be a gentleman in a more intensive sense of the word than is usual, I shouldn't be talking to you like this. Have a cigar." There was another long pause. The doctor debated quickly with himself what course to take. When he resumed, he used his rough weapon.

"You ought to know that my daughter will have very little in case of my death."—This time the young man rose entirely from his seat. The doctor smiled and waved him back. "And nothing until my death, which won't come while you are a young man. The world reports me well to do, and I am, but I am taxed by society heavily. I mean I have large demands on my income, and aside from certain properties that must be left in trust for other people and a modest provision for my wife and child, there isn't likely to be much. I tell you all this, partly because I like you, and partly because I think it is only fair. I don't think you are after money. But you must realize now that money will make a great difference in your career."

When Long moved hastily, the doctor smiled.

"I don't say that you should hunt a fortune, but you should keep out of the way of attractive women without fortune."

This time he gave Long an opportunity to vent his feelings. When he had finished, he began again quietly.

"What you say is singularly like what I said myself about nineteen years ago. I think I will tell you the story," and he proceeded coldly to give him an outline of his life. Long listened respectfully. At the close he said, "But the cases are not similar, exactly."

"No two human cases ever are, but the theme is the same. You might arrange a different compromise; it would be a compromise."

"Your difficulties were enormous! Why need I plan for such misfortunes?"

"You mean the outside affairs, the money? That might be arranged of course. There would remain my daughter, a subject which I can discuss with precision. She is in fair health, and while I live to look after her she will probably continue so. Her nerves are morbid, her egotism is excessive, her restlessness is abnormal. She is rather a brilliant girl, I think, and to me a very dear one. But her career needs to be guided, or some decided smash will come."

"You have no confidence in me?"

"The greatest. It is not her welfare only which I am considering, but yours. Besides, if she were normal or dull, not an exacting young American, yet she would be a woman. And as such her interests must be opposed to yours forever. Should you marry her, I would be forced to agree with her and oppose you wherever you stepped beyond conventionality."

Suddenly Long turned on his tormentor with a bold question.

"Your marriage you would not consider a failure, even under worse conditions?"

The doctor winced at this thrust, which he considered legitimate.

He had had his moments of doubt even in the thick of his loyalty to his wife and child when this question had tormented him. Miasmatic moments that come to firm men also, and make them dizzy with the thought of the mere waywardness of life. Had he been any better or wiser than Roper Ellwell? When the test of a vital passion had come he had acted like any other inconsiderate, purposeless young man, like any one with a chaotic will-less past!

But this temptation he had mastered, as he had mastered almost all the elements of his fate.

"That kind of a question can never be answered fairly. No one has the complete data. No! I can honestly say *no*. Yet it has altered my life profoundly, that I can say."

"Then why are you so pessimistic for me?"

"Because," the doctor replied, slowly, "such a marriage as mine has been, such a marriage as yours would be, is a career in itself. Beyond that *nothing*— understand, *nothing*."

"Love is a great career!"

"It is; but there is hardly a man I have ever known who could embrace it, and that only, for a lifetime. You could not, I think, and you would be miserable. It is a humble career though it is rich. The man who wins does not devote his life to an exacting passion for a neurotic woman. You are the man to win: go in."

The doctor rose.

"Now I must leave you to see a patient who has been waiting. Think—you don't love her, poor child; what do you know of love? You are putting your mind in order for love, and it will come quickly enough."

Long stared irresponsibly at the floor. "I am glad we have been able to talk this over without passion. You have not obliged me to use any coarse authority, or any influence except your own sane judgment. We have been unsentimental men. You have confessed to nothing more than a liking for a pretty girl. You have committed yourself to nothing."

The doctor paused, resting his hands firmly on the table between them. He read the young man's face eagerly, and he felt sure that he had gained his point.

"Now, go," he continued kindly, "and God-speed to you! Go in to win!"

He turned. Long rose mechanically as if ordered by a superior, opened the door, and disappeared into the dark hall. The doctor listened for the sound of his footsteps. When he heard the tread on the ground beneath the office window, he sighed and stepped out into the hall. His daughter was standing in the doorway at the farther end, as if looking for some one.

"Where is Mr. Long, papa?"

"He has gone."

The doctor's voice dwelt slightly on the last word. The girl glanced at him sharply, and then turned back into the lighted drawing-room.

"Dinner is waiting, Jarvis," Mrs. Thornton spoke from a lounge within the room. "Why didn't you keep Mr. Long?"

The doctor walked over to his wife and stood for a moment by her side. She smiled in further interrogation; the doctor bent and kissed her.

"Long didn't care to stay," he replied. Then he went back to his patient.

Lightning Source UK Ltd.
Milton Keynes UK
UKHW041629110820
367994UK00020B/1259